Nick Mack's Good Luck

MARA BERGMAN

ILLUSTRATED BY

JILL BARTON

WALKER
BOOKS

For Terri, Alan, Miki, Ellie,
Ethan and Shain
M.B.

For Maggie and Steve
and Katie and Max
J.B.

First published 2005 by Walker Books Ltd
87 Vauxhall Walk, London SE11 5HJ

6 8 10 9 7 5

Text © 2005 Mara Bergman
Illustrations © 2005 Jill Barton

The right of Mara Bergman and Jill Barton to be identified as author
and illustrator respectively of this work has been asserted by them in
accordance with the Copyright, Designs and Patents Act 1988

This book has been typeset in Bembo Educational

Printed and bound in China

British Library Cataloguing in Publication Data:
a catalogue record for this book
is available from the British Library

ISBN 978-1-84428-091-9

www.walker.co.uk

Four-Leaf Clovers

5

Nick's Luck

25

The Rainbow

45

Four-Leaf Clovers

Nick Mack collected things. He kept
them on a bookcase in his bedroom.
There were dinosaurs along the top
shelf, racing cars on the second shelf
and everything else on the bottom shelf:
used postage stamps, unusual stones,
seashells, and elastic bands for his
elastic-band ball.

Nick had lots of things, but more
than anything he wanted a pet.

7

All of his friends had pets.

Ethan had a rabbit.

Lee had a tortoise.

Shane had a
tank full of fish.

Ellie had Newton,
the best dog in the world.

Whenever Nick asked his mother
if he could have a pet, she said,
"Someday, Nick. Someday when
you're older."

But Nick was beginning to think that
someday was never day.

Nick liked it when Aunt Terri came to stay. She always brought her bag with the big bright flowers on it. She said it brought her good luck. Nick thought it brought him good luck too.

Every time Aunt Terri reached into the bag, she pulled out something special.

One time it was a T-shirt with a picture of a dinosaur on the front.

Another time it was an aeroplane that really flew.

When Nick Mack heard the flip-flap
of flip-flops coming up the path, he
knew his aunt was here.

"How's my favourite boy?"
said Aunt Terri when
Nick ran to greet her.

"Great!" he said,
and he gave
her a hug.

They went into the kitchen.

"How's my favourite sister?" Mum asked. "Have a good journey?"

"Yes," said Aunt Terri. "But I could do with a cold drink."

Everyone had a cold drink. It was a hot day.

"Let's see what I've brought for you, Nick," said Aunt Terri, reaching into her bag. "Hmmm … where did it go?"

Out came a mirror,

a book,

some clothes,

an umbrella

and a toothbrush.

That was all. "I am *so* sorry, Nick!
I must have forgotten it!"

Nick would have liked a present, but
it didn't matter that much.

Just then the baby started to cry.

"I'll be right back," said Mum,
though Nick knew she would be ages.

"Let's go to the park," Aunt Terri
said. "A walk will do me good after
all that driving."

"Yes, yes, yes!" Nick shouted.

"I'd better see to Annie!" called

Mum. "See you later."

The park had swings and slides,
picnic tables, and a wood for nature
walks and treasure hunts. Nick and
Aunt Terri ran to the great big field.

"You're fast, Nick!" said Aunt Terri.

Then she looked down and started
combing through the grass with her
fingers.

"What did you lose?" Nick asked.

"Nothing," said Aunt Terri. "I'm
looking for four-leaf clovers."

"That's easy," said Nick. "There
are millions of them."

But there weren't millions.
Or hundreds. Or even one!

There were lots of clovers with three
leaves, but not a single one with four.

"I think I've found one!"
said Aunt Terri. Then,
"Maybe not."

"There's one!"
said Nick.

And there was!
He picked it.
"You are one lucky
boy, Nick Mack!
I hope you'll share
your good luck with
your auntie."

When they returned home, Aunt Terri got out a dictionary. She put Nick's four-leaf clover inside it and smoothed down the leaves.

"This will help to keep your clover for ever," she said, "and your good luck too. Now it's time for me to help your mum."

First she went to put her sunglasses
back in her bag.

"What's this?" she said, holding up a
small parcel. "I must have remembered
it after all!" She handed the parcel to
Nick.

It seemed to Nick that his four-leaf
clover had brought him luck already.

Nick's Luck

Nick Mack had a special friend, Ellie.
Ellie Gold lived next door.
Ellie had a dog called Newton.
Nick and Ellie played with
Newton all the time.

Nick helped Ellie feed and
walk Newton.

He helped her wash and brush him.

Ellie was very good at sharing
Newton with Nick.

There was another reason why Ellie
was Nick's special friend. Ellie liked
collecting things too.

While Aunt Terri was at home helping Mum, Nick went round to Ellie's. Ellie and Newton were already at the door.

"Hi, Nick," said Ellie.

"Woof! Woof, woof!" said Newton.

Nick reached into his pocket, then gave Newton a dog treat. He always had a dog treat for Newton.

"My dad's taking us to the park," said Ellie. "But first Newton and I are going to practise some tricks. Want to help?"

Ellie and Nick took turns throwing
the special stick that Nick had found
during one of their nature walks.

Newton ran fast and jumped high
and brought the stick back quickly. He
did this a few times, then lay down by
Ellie's feet.

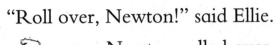

"Roll over, Newton!" said Ellie.
Newton rolled over.

"Paw," said Ellie.
Newton sat up and
gave Ellie his paw.

"Paw," said Nick.
Newton gave Nick
his paw as well.

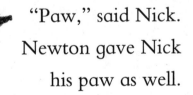

Then, because he loved to run,
Nick ran up and down Ellie's garden.
Newton ran up and down Ellie's
garden too.

Mr Gold opened the door and said,
"Are you ready, Ellie? Hello, Nick.
Why don't you ask your mum if you
can come to the park with us?"
So Nick did. And he could.

At the park Newton did a lot of
sniffing. He rolled in the grass.
Other people were out
with their dogs too –

Mrs Regent from
the post office,

and Jonny Smith
and Mark Burden
from school.

As they walked across the field Nick said, "I found a four-leaf clover right here yesterday."

"Really?" asked Ellie.

"You must be very lucky," said Mr Gold. "I've never found a four-leaf clover in my life! Have you made a wish?"

"Oh, yes," said Nick. Nick was always wishing. And he always wished for the same thing.

"I hope your wish comes true," said Mr Gold.

Suddenly Newton saw a squirrel –
and he was off!

"Newton! Newton!" Ellie and Nick
and Mr Gold called, but Newton kept
running. Then Nick had an idea. He
reached into his pocket and held up a
dog treat.

"*Newton!*" he called very loudly.

Newton turned, Newton looked and
Newton ran – fast – straight back to Nick.

"See," said Ellie. "Newton thinks he's
your dog too!"

On the way back to
Ellie's, Nick found three
elastic bands for his
elastic-band ball. It was
going to be the biggest in the world.

He found two feathers

and an unusual-
looking stone.

He would put them on his bookcase
when he got home.

Ellie found four acorns.

She also found two
small buttons

and an old key.

"I didn't know you liked keys," said
Nick.

"Neither did I," said Ellie, "but I
collect them now."

At home Ellie and Nick each gave
Newton another dog treat. "Even
though he was a bit naughty," said
Ellie. Then they brushed Newton's
fur until it was
silky and soft.

Afterwards Nick said, "I'd better go now. Thank you for having me."

Nick had lots to think about. He thought about Newton and Ellie, and how Ellie had said Newton thought he was Nick's dog too. He thought about them living next door. He thought about collecting things and also about friendship.

"I *am* lucky," said Nick to himself.
Then Nick Mack skipped back home.

The Rainbow

Nick Mack loved birthdays –
especially when they were his. He
also loved sunny days. But when
Nick Mack woke up on his
birthday, the sun was not shining.
The day was wet and cold.

Mum and Aunt Terri and Annie
came bouncing and singing into Nick's
room. "Happy birthday to you, happy
birthday to you…" Balloons came
bouncing in too.

Mum and Aunt Terri each gave
Nick a birthday kiss. Then they gave
him his presents.

Aunt Terri gave Nick
a racing car for
his racing car
collection and
a shiny box.

"When I saw this, I had to get it for
you!" she said. On the box it said:

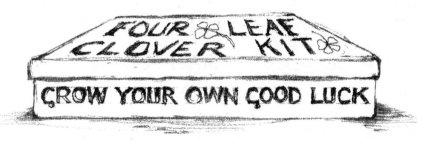

FOUR LEAF CLOVER KIT

GROW YOUR OWN GOOD LUCK

Mum gave Nick a great big box of
sticks and bricks and nuts and bolts to
build things.

She also gave him a box full of
drawers. "That's to help you organize
all your collections," she said.

Annie's present was a cuddly monkey

that laughed when you squeezed its
paw. Everyone else laughed too.

Nick Mack loved his presents. But
even though he had wished and wished
and wished for a pet of his own, he still
didn't have one. Suddenly he thought of
Newton, and he smiled.

"Time for your birthday breakfast!"
said Mum. "What would you like?"
Nick wanted everything – cereal and
eggs and toast and a bowl full
of strawberries.

After a while Nick asked, "Can we still go to the farm?" The farm was to be his birthday outing.

"Of course," said Mum. "It's not raining hard. We'll just have to wear our macs, Nick Mack!"

After breakfast Nick went next door
to get Ellie.

"Happy birthday, Nick," said Nick's
special friend.

"Woof! Woof, woof!" said Newton,
Nick's special dog. Nick stroked
Newton's head and gave him a
dog treat.

"Are we going now?" asked Ellie.

"Yes, yes, yes!" said Nick.

McAlan's Farm was only a short car
ride away. When they got there, Mum
bought a few small bags
of animal feed.

"Imagine having
a goat!" said
Nick as they fed
the goats.

"Imagine
having a horse!"
he said as they
fed the horses.

They stroked
the rabbits,

then went into a barn
and watched newborn chicks
hopping under bright lights.

KITTENS
FREE
TO GOOD
HOMES

Afterwards Aunt Terri bought everyone an ice cream.

Outside the shop, a sign leaning against the gatepost said:

KITTENS FREE
To GOOD HOMES

A boy sat on a big stone. He held a box wriggling with kittens.

Nick loved them straight away.

"Aren't they sweet," said Mum.

Mum had always said that dogs were too much work, and she didn't want a rabbit or a tortoise or a tank full of fish. But Mum liked kittens – and she liked cats too.

Nick stroked the grey one with the white patch on its back. "You can pick her up," said the boy. "She's the smallest. We call her Lucky."

"We call Nick lucky, too!" said Ellie. She almost told the boy about Nick finding the four-leaf clover, but she decided not to.

Mum had a word with Aunt Terri.
She looked at the kittens again and
then went into the shop.

When she came out she said,
"Happy birthday,
Nick Mack!
Lucky is all
yours."

Just then the sun came out and a rainbow stretched from one end of the field to the other.

"You're supposed to make a wish," said Mum.

For the first time ever, Nick didn't
feel like making a wish.

All his wishes had already come true.